This book belongs to...

....

....

JUNGLE TALES
Monkey Mayhem

Written by Ronne Randall
Illustrated by Jacqueline East

Mickey and Maxine Monkey
had finished breakfast and were
rushing off to play.

"Be careful!" called their mum.
"And DON'T make too much noise!"

"Okay," the cheeky monkeys promised.

"WHEEEE," screeched Mickey.

"WA-HOOOO!" hollered Maxine.

The noise echoed through the whole jungle. Mickey and Maxine just couldn't be quiet!

KA-THUNK!

Mickey landed on a branch.

KA-CLUNK!

Maxine landed beside him.

KER-AACK!

"OOOHHH, NOOOO!"

the monkeys hollered, as
the branch snapped in two.

"YI-I-IKES!"

they shrieked, as they went
tumbling down, down, down.

KERTHUMMPP! SPROI-OI-OING!

The jungle shook, as the two monkeys crashed to the ground, then sprang to their feet.

"YIPPPEEEEEE!" the monkeys cheered, brushing themselves off.

"That was so much **FUN!**" exclaimed Maxine. "Let's go get Chico Chimp and see if he wants to do it, too!"

Chattering as they went, the two monkeys scrambled back up to the tree tops.

"Hey, Chico! Come and play with us!" they bellowed, as they swung through the branches, towards the chimps' house.

All through the jungle, animals shook their heads and covered their ears. Couldn't anyone keep those naughty, noisy monkeys quiet?

Chico Chimp was soon ready to play with his friends. The three of them had a great time, swinging, tumbling and bouncing together.

Then, they spotted a coconut palm.

"Hey!" shouted Chico. "Let's get some coconuts!"

"Great!" said Maxine. "Last one up the tree is a rotten banana!"

But before they got to the tree, Grandpa Gorilla stopped them. He glared at them.

"Clear off, you mischief-makers," he said. "You've given everyone enough headaches for one day. My grandson, Gulliver, is asleep by the river and if you wake him up, I will be very, *very* upset!"

"Sorry," whispered Maxine, looking down at the ground. Everyone in the jungle knew it was a big mistake to upset Grandpa Gorilla!

"We'll be quiet," the three friends promised.

Mickey, Maxine and Chico started to wander away. Then, Mickey said, "Let's just climb the tree. Maybe we can do that quietly."

"Okay," the others agreed, half-heartedly.

"It's better than doing nothing," said Maxine.

From their perch up among the coconuts, the three friends could see out over the whole jungle.

They saw Jerome Giraffe teaching his son, Jeremy, to nibble leaves...

... and they saw Portia Parrot giving her daughter, Penelope, her first flying lesson.

And right below them, they saw Gulliver Gorilla, sleeping peacefully by the river.

And, **uh-oh!** They saw something else, too! Claudia Crocodile was nearby. She was snapping her big, sharp teeth – and heading straight for Gulliver!

The three friends didn't think twice.
Maxine shouted, **"GET UP, GULLIVER!**

GET UP RIGHT NOW!"

At the same time, Mickey and Chico began throwing coconuts at Claudia.

THWACK! went the coconuts.

SMACK! they went, right on Claudia's hard, crocodile head.

"OWW-WOOWW!" moaned Claudia. **"OWW-WOW OWW-WOW!"**

All the noise woke Gulliver. The little gorilla
sat up, looked around and ran to his grandpa,
who was hurrying towards the river.

Then, he saw Claudia swimming away and
he realised what had happened. He grabbed
Gulliver and gave him a great, big, gorilla hug.
"I'm so glad you're safe!" he said.

Maxine, Mickey and Chico came down from the tree.

"Sorry about the noise," Chico said.

By this time, all the other gorillas had gathered round and so had most of the other jungle animals.

"What's all the commotion about?" asked Jerome Giraffe.

"Yes, what's going on?" squawked Portia Parrot.

"These three youngsters are heroes," said Grandpa. "They saved my grandson from being eaten by Claudia Crocodile!"

Everyone cheered and Mrs Monkey and Mrs Chimp beamed with pride.

"You deserve a reward," said Grandpa Gorilla. "And I think your reward should be... "

All the other animals held their breath.

PEEEEE!"
cheered Mickey, Maxine and Chico. Their grins were almost as wide as the river!

"OH, NO!"
all the other animals groaned together, but they were all smiling, too.

This is a Bright Sparks Book, this edition published in 2002
BRIGHT SPARKS, Queen Street House, 4 Queen Street,
Bath BA1 1HE, UK

Copyright © PARRAGON 2001

Created and produced by THE COMPLETE WORKS

Printed in China

ISBN 1-84250-585-8